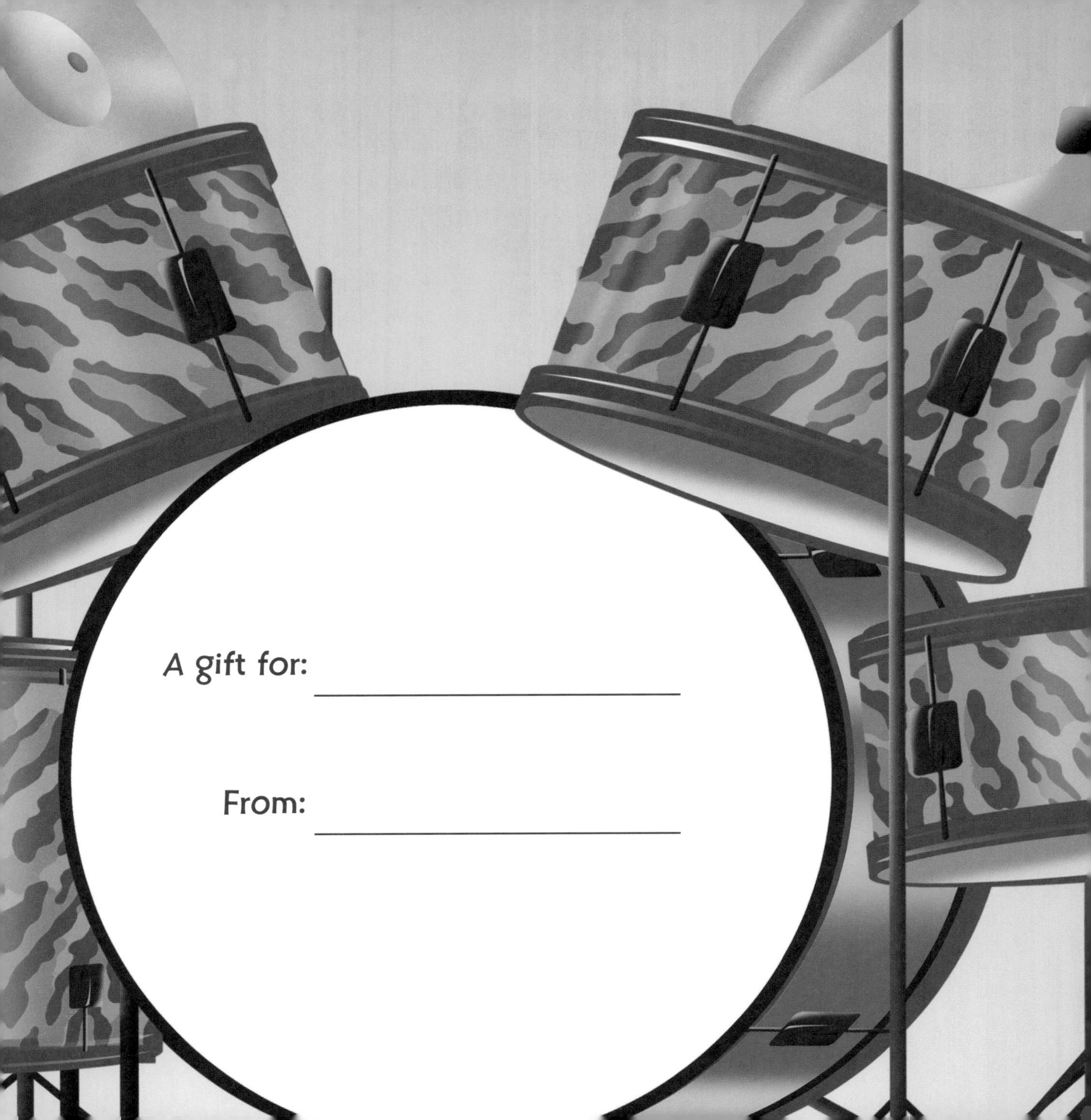
A gift for: ______________________
From: ______________________

The Watering Hole Journal

Published by Hallmark Gift Books, a division of Hallmark Cards, Inc., Kansas City, MO 64141
Visit us on the Web at www.Hallmark.com.

Editor: Jared Smith
Art Director: Kevin Swanson
Designer and Production Artist: Dan Horton

ISBN: 978-1-59530-464-3
VTD5016

Printed and bound in China
SEP11

The Zoo York Times

Eddie Ape at the top of the charts

BENNY'S BIG BREAK

by ERIN CANTY

illustrated by
JACK PULLAN

Hallmark
GIFT BOOKS

WINNER

Benny loved everything about living in the jungle. There were friendly animals to play with, yummy foods to eat, and new places to explore. Each day was an exciting adventure. But while the other young animals were busy playing, Benny was busy dreaming.

Benny daydreamed about being a rock star. He fantasized about bright lights, sold-out stadiums, and mobs of fans screaming his name. Even though it was just make-believe, Benny knew that somehow, someday, he'd be famous . . . just like his big brother, Eddie.

the
WILD
BUNCH

Animals near and far knew Eddie Ape. He was a drummer for the most rockin' band this side of the watering hole. They were stars. And Eddie's star shined the brightest of all.

Rolling Banana
Eddie Ape
Rocks On!

Zoo York Times
ddie Ape at the
p of the charts
WINNER

Benny enjoyed watching his big brother rehearse. Today's practice was special. It was the last one before the Jungle Talent Show.

After practicing for a long time, the band finally finished. Eddie wiped sweat from his brow. "I'm going to cool off at the lagoon," he said.

Benny tiptoed over to the drum set. He looked to the left. He peeked to the right. He was all alone.

"Eddie won't mind if I get a better look," he thought.

Benny inched closer, admiring the shiny knobs and clasps.

"They're almost too wonderful NOT to play," he said to himself. "And Eddie always says, practice makes perfect."

Benny lifted himself onto Eddie's stool, picked up the drumsticks, and lightly tapped each drum. The shimmery sound of the cymbal and the deep thump of the bass drum sent his imagination spinning.

He closed his eyes. He could almost hear the roar of screaming fans. He could nearly see the lights dim over the crowded arena.

He started to play. He pounded rhythms left and right. *Rat-a-tat-tat!* The make-believe audience showered him with applause. Benny was unstoppable. But then . . .

CRASH!!

"Oh, no!" Benny cried. "Eddie will never let me near his drums again!"

But then he got an idea.

"This tear isn't so big," Benny said. "I'll just have to fix it. The drum will be good as new in no time." Feeling determined, he set about looking for a way to fix the drum.

The skipping rocks by the watering hole? There were so many to choose from, but they were all too small to cover the tear. *Perhaps some vines from the trees?* They were extra strong, but they were way too high for him to reach.

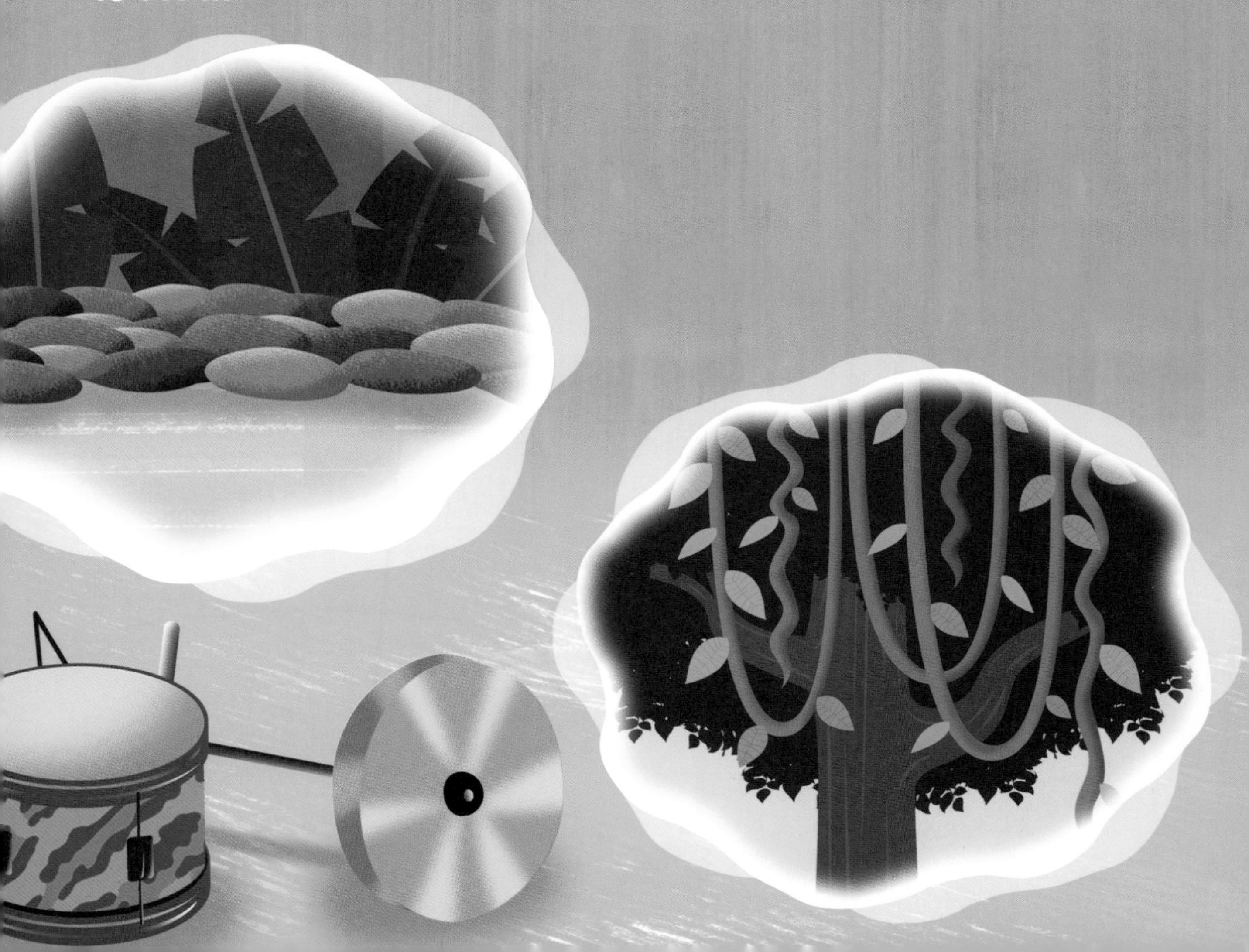

Benny searched high and low. Then he spotted it!

"The banana tree! Of course!" He walked over to the lush, swaying branches. *A few banana peels would cover the hole perfectly!*

Benny peeled a banana and popped it in his mouth. *Munch, munch, munch.*

"Mmm. This is my tastiest idea yet," he said, chomping on the sweet fruit.

Benny ate one banana...

then two...

then three...

But by the fourth banana,
he wasn't feeling so well.
And he still didn't have enough
peels to repair the hole.

Just then, Eddie came back. Bananas and peels were tossed about everywhere. And in the middle of the mess was his broken drum.

"What happened here, buddy?" Eddie asked.

"I wanted to be a rock star like you," said Benny.

Eddie examined the drum set. Then he looked at Benny, unable to hide his smile. Soon, he erupted into a booming laugh.

Benny scratched his head, surprised by his big brother's fit of laughing. "What's so funny?" he asked.

"You're more like me than you know, little bro," Eddie said. "When I was small like you, I broke Papa Ape's drum. I bet you were busy daydreaming, just like I was."

Benny nodded with a grin.

"You'll be a real star someday, Benny. But you'd better leave the drumming to me for now," Eddie said. "But there is something I need your help with."

Eddie handed Benny a pair of maracas. Benny gave them a shake. *Chicka-chicka-chicka.* He was a natural!

"Now, let's see if all that practicing paid off!" Eddie said.

And it did!

Today
ow Winners!
FIRST
PLACE

If you have enjoyed this book
we would love to hear from you.
Please send your comments to:
Hallmark Book Feedback
P.O. Box 419034
Mail Drop 215
Kansas City, MO 64141
Or e-mail us at:
booknotes@hallmark.com